# TALES FROM THE
# Africa
# PLAINS

# TALES FROM THE
# *African*
# PLAINS

### RETOLD BY ANNE GATTI

## Paintings by
## Gregory Alexander

◇ ◇ ◇

Dutton Children's Books

NEW YORK

THIS BOOK IS DEDICATED TO MY FRIEND,
MARGARET ADAMS,
WHO INTRODUCED ME TO AFRICA.
THANK YOU.
*G.A.*

TO THOMAS AND GEORGIA
*A.G.*

Text copyright © 1994 by Pavilion Books Ltd.
Illustrations copyright © 1994 by Gregory Alexander
All rights reserved.
CIP Data is available.
First published in the United States 1995 by
Dutton Children's Books,
a division of Penguin Books USA Inc.
375 Hudson Street, New York, New York 10014
Originally published in Great Britain 1994 by
Pavilion Books Limited, London
Typography by Adrian Leichter
Produced by Mandarin Offset, Printed in China
1 3 5 7 9 10 8 6 4 2
First American Edition
ISBN 0-525-45282-6

# CONTENTS

◈

# THE BOY AND
# NYANGE THE COW

THERE WAS ONCE A BOY WHO SPENT HIS DAYS guarding his father's cattle, out on the plains. He was a very good herdsman, and the animals obeyed and trusted him.

The boy's mother had died when he was only a baby, and he had no older brothers or sisters. So it was his responsibility to take care of his father's house. When he arrived home after a long day in the hot fields, there was always more work to do.

The boy's father was a very bad-tempered, mean-spirited man. He did not care that all the work prevented his son from making friends and going to the dances that were held in nearby villages. The other young people of the Kikuyu tribe felt sorry for the boy. Many of the girls thought him handsome and would have liked to get to know him. But he was always either grazing his cattle or cooking and sewing indoors.

The boy did have one friend, though—a cow named Nyange. Nyange had a dark, glossy coat and magnificent white horns. She seemed to understand that the boy was lonely, so she grazed close by to keep him company. Whenever he wandered away from her, she would moo and moo until he came back. The boy fed her tidbits from his own meals whenever he could, and when he went to the clay mines he always brought her back chunks of the salty clay as a special treat.

The boy often talked to Nyange as if she were human. He didn't really expect her to understand, but it was good to be able to tell her his feelings. One day, forgetting that she was only a cow, he said:

"Move over a bit, Nyange, you're blocking my view of that group of cows over by the bushes."

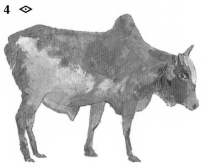

Nyange took a few steps to the left and went on grazing. The boy was amazed. Perhaps she just moved to get some more grass, he thought. I'll say something else and see what happens.

"Nyange, go over to the bushes and tell those cows to come back here. It's time to go home," he said.

Nyange lifted her head and looked at him as if to say, "Certainly, if that's what you want." Then she ambled over to the other cows, mooed at them, and led them back to the boy.

He couldn't believe it: a cow that understood human speech, and it was *his* cow. He threw his arms around Nyange and shouted with happiness. It didn't matter that his legs were tired or that the black flies had been biting him. He now had a very special friend, and he would keep her a secret from his father.

When he got home, he watered the cattle and put them into the kraal.* Then he went indoors as if nothing had happened. As usual, his father was just on his way out for the evening and had left behind lots of chores. But that night the boy didn't mind so much. He was too excited about his extraordinary cow.

When the boy went to let out the cattle the next day, he could hear Nyange mooing louder than all the others. She didn't stop until he went over to her and scratched her behind the ears. She licked his hands and swished her tail as he led her out, and together they led the herd to the plains.

A few years went by and the boy grew very tall and strong. Nyange still helped him herd the rest of the cattle, and he still talked to her and brought her salty clay whenever he could. But he was restless. His father was away from home most of the time, making merry in village after village, and the boy was very lonely. He could hear the sounds of loud singing, feet stamping, and drums beating from across the plains and he longed to be dancing with all the other young people.

One day he had an idea. He would ask Nyange to look after the cattle while he went to a dance at a nearby village.

Nyange swished her tail in agreement. The boy ran most of the way to the

*kraal*: a fenced enclosure

dance, where he found that the other young people were delighted to see him. He talked and danced. He told them that a friend of his was looking after his cattle. From time to time, he would remember the cattle and wonder if they were safe. Someone mentioned that cattle thieves from a nearby camp of Masai warriors had raided several herds. But the boy was having such a good time that he stayed at the party until dusk.

As the sun was setting he headed back toward his cattle. As soon as he spotted them safely grazing, with Nyange keeping a watchful eye on them, he sang out,

> *Nyange! Nyange!*
> *Round them up, bring them in, Nyange.*
> *Night has come, Nyange.*
> *Let's go home, Nyange.*

Nyange swished her tail and rounded up the cattle, herding them toward the boy.

The boy was happier than he had ever been. The cattle were safe, he'd had a wonderful time, and now he could be like the other boys and girls and go to dances regularly.

And so he did, and he became a very good dancer. On days when there were no dances, he would visit the new friends he had made. As the months went by, he began to spend more and more time with one particular girl who had beautiful eyes and wore rows and rows of brightly colored beads. But at sunset, he always returned to his cattle and greeted Nyange with the special song before leading the cattle home. He told nobody about his extraordinary friend.

One day he went to a dance in a village several miles away and stayed there all day. It was almost dark by the time he got back to the spot where he had left Nyange and the herd. He sang his usual song, but nothing happened. There was no moo from Nyange, no clang of cowbells, no clump of hooves coming toward him.

Maybe they've wandered over the hill, he thought. And he ran as fast as he

could to the hilltop and sang again. Still nothing happened. He was now very worried. What if some Masai raiders had stolen Nyange and his herd while he was at the dance? He could never have heard the cattle bellowing from that distance. What would his father say? How would they survive? How would he ever be able to pay for a wife?

He hurried back through the dusty scrub to the place he had last seen the cattle. He looked on the ground for clues to what might have happened. He noticed long footprints next to a flurry of hoofprints and then he saw something red caught on a branch of a shrub. It was a piece of red cloth that looked as if it had been torn off a cloak.

"Masai!" he whispered into the night. He knew that the Masai liked to paint their hair red and wear red clothes.

The boy suddenly felt afraid. What should he do? If he followed the hoofprints and caught up with the fierce Masai warriors, they would probably kill him with their long spears. If he didn't try to find the cattle, his father would give him a terrible beating. And then he remembered Nyange. Poor Nyange, he thought. A prisoner in a strange country. Perhaps they won't even give her enough to eat and drink.

That decided it. Even if he could save only Nyange, he must try to find the cattle. Although it would have been wise to go home and fetch a war spear and shield, he decided not to waste any more time and set off in the dark, armed only with the short spear and dagger that he normally carried in case lions or hyenas attacked his herd.

All night long he followed the tracks, through bushes that scratched him and over stones that cut his feet, up steep mountains and across rivers. Sometimes he stopped to catch his breath, but after a minute or so he would imagine that he heard Nyange's deep mooing and would set off again, determined to rescue her.

At dawn, he climbed yet another mountain. By the time he reached the top, which was surprisingly flat, the sun was beating down and he was longing for a drink. He looked down and saw a grassy valley beneath him. Dotted all along it, like brown pools in a swamp, were herds of cattle grazing. There must have been hundreds of cows, some brown, some white, some big and strong, others skinny and scrawny. In the middle, smoke drifted up from several fires, and the boy could make out a Masai camp.

He sat down and stared at the scene below him. Tall men, with long plaited hair that glinted red in the bright light, moved among the cattle. Now and then he could see them poking the animals with the butt end of their long spears to keep the herds together. He shaded his eyes to see if he could pick out his herd. Suddenly he spotted a cow with beautiful white horns. From where he was sitting, the herd she was with looked about the same size as his own. It must be Nyange, he thought. His cattle were close to the base of the mountain, but there was no point in going down to rescue them in broad daylight. He would have to wait until nightfall.

Patiently, the boy watched the Masai camp all day. In his mind, he tried to work out a plan to steal back

his herd. He didn't stir, even to get a drink. As the distant hilltops turned a beautiful reddish gold, the Masais started to gather around the cookfires to eat their evening meal. They left only a few warriors to guard the herds. Soon the boy heard voices and smelled the tantalizing odor of roasted meat.

The words of the Masai songs drifted up the mountain in the still night. The

Kikuyu people were useless, chanted the warriors. They let the women cook their food, and they didn't know the first thing about cattle or how to look after them. The Kikuyu didn't deserve to own cattle. The Masai had a right to take cattle from the worthless Kikuyu.

The boy was furious to hear his people so insulted, but the loud chantings of the warriors had given him an idea. He waited a few more hours till the valley grew silent except for the occasional clanking of a cowbell. The Masai were sleeping. He climbed down the mountain toward the valley as quietly as he could and stood on a rock near the bottom. Softly he sang,

> *Nyange! Nyange!*
> *Round them up, bring them in, Nyange.*
> *Night has come, Nyange.*
> *Let's go home, Nyange.*

Immediately he heard a cow mooing softly. Could it be Nyange? Had she heard and understood him? He sang his greeting song again. This time he was sure that the answering moo was Nyange's, and he stood there, his heart beating very fast as he listened to the sound of hooves cutting through the grass. The cows were moving in his direction, and there seemed to be lots of them— many more than he was expecting.

He didn't have to wait long before he saw Nyange's magnificent white horns approaching. He jumped off his rock and ran to greet her. "Nyange! Nyange! Are you all right? You are so clever," he whispered. "Can you make the journey back home?"

Nyange put her head down for the boy to scratch behind her ears and then she licked his hand. He understood. She was saying "yes" to both his questions. He quickly explained the route he was going to take, and asked her to lead the rest of the huge herd that was appearing in front of him. He knew they would follow her.

He started up the mountain. Halfway to the top, he then cut to the side so that the cattle would not tire too quickly from the steep climb. To his surprise the cattle didn't bellow or call, as they normally did when traveling. Clever Nyange must have warned them to be silent.

It was only when the boy started to head around the other side of the mountain that the Masai guards awoke to find that all of the cattle closest to the base of the mountain had gone. They roared and shouted, waking all the others, and frantically looked to see where the cows had vanished. Then one of the guards spotted a light-colored cow at the back of the herd that was scrambling up the mountainside. Several of the warriors ran after it, shouting and shaking their spears. They ran like the wind and soon caught up with the last of the escaping herd. But the cows kicked out and bellowed as if they had gone mad, and several of the Masai were knocked down and injured. Then, still bellowing like raging bulls, the stragglers charged ahead and caught up with the rest.

When the guards saw how fierce the cattle were, they went back down to the valley and asked their elders what to do. The elders listened to the story and said that the cattle must belong to the great god E-Ngai, and that he must have called the animals back to his kingdom in the sky. E-Ngai was angry with the Masai, the elders explained, and would kill any warriors who followed the cattle up the mountain. As the first rays of the morning sun lit up the mountaintop, the elders fell to their knees and begged E-Ngai to forgive them for stealing his cattle.

So the Masai thieves decided not to follow the cattle. After a few hours, the boy realized that for some reason he was not being chased, and he stopped at the bank of a river. He bent down and took a long drink, and so did all the cattle. Now for the first time he could see how many creatures he was herding—there were at least three hundred of them, maybe more, swishing their tails and grazing peacefully at the water's edge.

After an hour's rest, the boy forded the river with Nyange right behind him and the long train of cattle behind her, all obediently sloshing through the water and trudging on toward the boy's home plains. He looked back and felt proud and excited: This was the greatest herd he had ever seen, and they were all obeying him. He led them at a steady pace, stopping every couple of hours to let them eat and drink.

It was midday on the following day when they climbed the hill overlooking the boy's village. As they crossed the stretch of scrub that led to his home, the cloud of dust surrounding them grew longer and longer as more cattle trod on the dry soil. It hid most of the herd from view. The villagers, who had heard the rumble of the approaching footsteps, stood and gaped. As the boy drew closer, they could see more and more cattle emerging from the cloud, as if by magic. The boy's father heard the commotion and joined his neighbors. He watched his son confidently leading this great army of cattle. For once he was speechless. At last he strode out to welcome his son home, and as he did so the women of the village sang out their traditional welcome:

"Aaari-ririri-ri!"

Father and son greeted each other and the rest of the villagers gathered around to hear the boy's story. The boy was thrilled to see that the girl with the beautiful eyes was standing at the front of the crowd and smiling. He told his tale about the Masai raid, how Nyange had saved his cattle, and how he had made his father a rich man by adding so many cattle to the herd.

When the boy had finished, the father, who was bursting with pride over his brave and clever son, announced that he was throwing a feast for all the villagers in celebration of the boy's return. He then turned to the boy and said,

"Son, you may now have the wife of your own choice. I will offer however many cattle are required."

"Father, I have already chosen my bride, if she will have me," answered the boy, and he walked over to the girl with the beautiful eyes.

She smiled and thanked him, and said yes, she would very much like to marry him. Then she walked over to Nyange, who was standing patiently at the head of the herd, and took off one of her bead necklaces. She draped it across Nyange's forehead, from ear to ear.

"Thank you," she whispered, "for bringing back my husband-to-be, safe and sound."

# THE WOMAN
# AND THE BIRD

ONE DAY A WOMAN TOOK UP HER AX AND went into the forest to cut down a banana tree. As she started to chip at the trunk, a bird swooped down from the upper branches and circled frantically around her head. The woman stopped chopping and watched as the bird flew up and lighted on a nest that was wedged in a fork of the tree. There it perched, fluttering its wings and squawking loudly.

"Oh, stop that racket!" the woman shouted, and she continued chopping until the tree began to topple. Just in time, the woman jumped back as the thick branches crashed onto the ground. But the nest flew out of the tree, and the eggs that the bird had been hatching were smashed into tiny pieces.

As the woman bent down to gather some bananas, she heard a female voice coming from the tangle of green near her feet.

"You shouldn't have killed my unborn chicks, woman of no feeling! You'll regret this one day."

The woman laughed when she realized that it was the bird speaking to her.

"Ha! What will you do to me? Peck me to pieces?"

And with that, the woman turned her back and sauntered home, carrying a load of bananas on her head.

Some months later, this same woman gave birth to a baby boy. As was the custom, her husband killed a ram for the naming ceremony. Many friends and relatives were invited, and when all the crowds had gathered, a boy called Waigwaini and a girl called Njoki were sent to fetch the pure springwater that would be needed for the ritual.

When the children arrived at the spring with their calabashes, they saw a magnificent bird perched in a tree. They had never seen such a beautiful creature in all their lives: Its brilliant tail feathers, spread out like a delicate fan, appeared to be decorated with rows of glittering jewels. As they stared at this magical vision, wondering if it could be real, the bird started to sing. Then it slowly hopped along the branch, swung upside down, and righted itself again. It danced its way back to them in the same fashion, fluttering its wings in rhythm to the steps. The children were mesmerized and forgot all about the water they were supposed to fetch.

When Waigwaini and Njoki had been gone a fair while, the woman's husband sent another boy to hurry them back. But as soon as he arrived at the spring and saw the bird, he too sat down beside Waigwaini and Njoki and watched.

More time passed and the woman and her husband were becoming very impatient.

"For goodness's sake," cried the woman, "what are those children doing? Why haven't they brought back the water?"

This time the husband asked his grown-up cousin to go in search of the children. As the man walked along, he called, "Waigwaini! Njoki! Where are you?" There was no reply, but in the distance a voice was singing:

> Come over here, to the spring, to hear me sing,
> Come join Waigwaini and Njoki at my dancing show.

The man found the children sitting on the ground and staring into a tree. As soon as he looked up and saw the bird's shimmering feathers, he felt his knees bend and he too sat down and was mesmerized.

By this time, the woman and her husband were becoming very worried indeed and decided that the rest of the party should go in search of the children and cousin together. Only the woman would stay behind with her new baby boy.

The woman waited alone for what seemed like ages. She ran out to the track every few minutes to see if anyone was coming. Finally she could not stand it any longer. With her baby sleeping in the house, she set off toward the spring. As she approached, she was astonished to see all her family sitting silently on the ground, staring at a fantastical bird. Suddenly the bird flew away, heading

*calabash: the dried shell of a large, rounded fruit

toward the village, and the spell was broken. The children and adults all looked at one another with puzzled faces.

"Why are you sitting there? Why haven't you fetched the water for the ceremony?" the woman asked each one in turn.

But no one could answer her, not even her husband. The children hurriedly scooped up some water and the whole party started back for the house. When they reached the edge of the village, Waigwaini suddenly shouted, "Look! Up on the roof! It's the bird. And there's something in its beak."

Sure enough, standing on the roof of the woman's house was the bird. It held a cloth-covered bundle in its beak.

The woman let out a piercing scream and ran toward the house.

"My baby!" she cried. "It has stolen my baby!"

When she got closer, the woman recognized that the bird was the same one whose nest and eggs she had destroyed in the forest. She burst into tears and got down on her knees.

"Please, please, bird," she pleaded, "spare my baby. I know I ignored you when you tried to save your chicks. I didn't realize you had a mother's feelings, just like me. I was very wrong. I'll do anything you ask, but please spare my baby."

Anxiously, the crowd watched, waiting to see what would happen. The men realized there was no point in flinging stones or trying to shoot the bird, for they might hurt the baby by accident. They were very surprised when the bird suddenly put down its bundle and began to speak.

"Woman, what you have said is true. We birds do have feelings, just like humans, and my chicks are as precious to me as your baby is to you. If you promise that from now on you will always be kind to birds and to the other animals of the forest, I will return your baby."

"Oh, sweet bird! How can I thank you?" The woman clapped her hands. "Of course I will be kind to all animals, and I will make sure that my children and other people are too. Please forgive me for having been so thoughtless before."

Having received the woman's promise, the bird flew down from the roof and laid the baby at her feet. It then took off again into the green of the forest.

The woman picked up her baby, who was still sleeping soundly, and the naming ceremony began with much rejoicing.

# THE CROCODILE, THE BOY, AND THE KIND DEED

◈

DIASSIGUE THE CROCODILE HAD SPENT THE whole day sleeping in the hot sun of the grasslands. He was crawling back through the marsh to his hole, which was under the bank of one of the many crisscrossing channels, when he heard the sound of female voices. Several women were chatting as they returned home with their calabashes full of water.

Diassigue crouched low, squashing his fat belly rather uncomfortably, and listened. The women were discussing something terrible that had happened earlier in the day: The king's young daughter had fallen into the water and drowned. The king had ordered the channels to be drained, they said, so that he could find her body.

Diassigue knew what that meant. He waited until they were out of sight, then turned around and began to walk in the direction from which he had just come. He moved at a surprisingly brisk pace, considering the size of his belly. By nightfall, he was deep in the grasslands, many miles from the village.

The next morning, the channels were drained, as the women had predicted, and all the crocodiles who lived in them were killed. The child's body was found in the hole belonging to the oldest crocodile, and the unhappy king made arrangements for her funeral.

Later that day, a boy from the village was sent off to fetch firewood. He was strolling along, watching a flock of weaverbirds making strange patterns in the sky, when he nearly stepped on Diassigue, who was sunning himself in the grass. The boy, who was called Gone, recognized Diassigue straightaway and was very surprised to see him so far from home.

"What are you doing here, Diassigue?" he asked.

"Gone, my son," said the crocodile eagerly. "I am so lucky to see you! I came out here for a bit of peace and quiet and now I have lost my bearings. But you can take me back home!"

"But, Diassigue," Gone replied, "your home has gone. The king drained the marsh."

Diassigue pretended to look astonished and then breathed a long sigh of resignation.

"Oh, well, I suppose I'll have to make a new home down by the river. But I couldn't possibly walk all the way there on my lame foreleg. You'll have to carry me, Gone."

Gone had never heard before about Diassigue's lame leg, but he felt sorry for the crocodile and so promised to help.

The boy remembered that he had seen a straw mat drying on a bush, so he went back and borrowed it. Then he cut some lianas* in the forest and returned to Diassigue. He rolled the big crocodile in the mat, tied up the bundle with the lianas, and heaved the weighty load onto his head. At first he staggered under the size of it and walked as if he had drunk too much beer.

"Steady on, Gone, my boy," came Diassigue's muffled voice from above. "You're making me seasick."

Gone walked on, a bit steadier as he grew used to the weight. But this was still the heaviest load he had ever carried, and he felt as if his neck might snap under the strain. But his legs kept striding until he reached the riverbank.

*liana: a ropelike vine

"There!" he panted as he lowered his bundle and cut the lianas. "Your new home."

Diassigue stretched out his legs and said, "Pretty bumpy ride, my friend. And now I find my wretched leg has gone to sleep. Could you just carry me into the water? I'll be fine once I'm afloat."

Gone picked up the mat once more and waded in up to his knees. He was just about to lower Diassigue into the water when the crocodile said, "No, no, a little farther out, please. Not enough depth here for me to swim properly."

Gone walked on. The water was soon up to his chest. He stopped to unload Diassigue when the crocodile interrupted once again.

"Go up to your shoulders, if you don't mind. Then I can just slide off."

Gone waded a little farther, then bent his head as Diassigue slid into the water. The boy turned to wade back to the bank when suddenly he felt something squeezing his arm painfully.

"Wooyeeyayo!" he shrieked. But Diassigue had a firm grip on Gone's arm, and the more the boy struggled, the tighter the crocodile clenched his jaws. "Let me go!" yelled Gone.

"I'm sorry, son," growled Diassigue through his teeth. "It's the law of the jungle. I'm very hungry—famished, actually—and you are a convenient meal. I can't possibly let you go."

"But, Diassigue!" Gone gasped, half in pain and half in fright. "I've just done something kind for you. Are you going to repay me by being so horrible and unkind?"

"Certainly I am. Didn't you know, Gone, a kind deed is repaid by a wicked one?"

"But that's not true!" replied Gone. "You just made that up. Everyone knows a kind deed is repaid by another kind deed."

"No, Gone. I'm afraid you have it all wrong," replied Diassigue impatiently.

"Oh, no, I haven't," said Gone. "Let's ask some others and see what they say!"

"All right, all right," snapped Diassigue, "but if the first three agree with me, you end up in my belly."

Just then a bony old cow ambled up to the water to have a drink. Diassigue called out to her from the middle of the river.

"Nagg, my friend, you're so wise and so venerable, I'm sure you can solve a problem for us. Tell us, how should a good deed be rewarded—by a kind deed or a wicked deed?"

"Oh, that's easy!" answered Nagg the Cow. "A wicked one. Shall I tell you how I know? When I was young and strong and gave my master plenty of milk and many calves, I was well looked after. After grazing each day, I was given bran and millet and a cake of salt to lick. My master's son rubbed me down and washed me. He never raised his stick to me because he knew he'd get a beating if he did. But now that I'm old and can't provide milk or calves, everything's changed. I am never taken to the field to feed on the juicy grasses. Instead, the boy drives me from the kraal in the morning with a stick and I wander and wander, looking for food. My coat gets caked with dirt and dust, but I'm never washed down or rubbed."

Nagg had said enough. She tried to flick away a biting insect from her hollowed back and headed off toward the grasslands, her head drooping between her shoulderblades.

Diassigue was delighted.

"Gone, my boy, did you hear that? Now let's see if we can get another opinion."

As he spoke, another animal approached the river. It was Fass the Horse. Like Nagg, he was old and thin and his lips trembled as he bent down to drink.

"Fass, my friend," called out Diassigue. "Gone and I were wondering if we could ask your opinion about something. You have lived a long and useful life. Tell us, how should a good deed be rewarded—by a kind deed or a wicked deed?"

Fass cleared his throat a couple of times and then he spoke.

"No doubt about it, a good deed is always rewarded by a wicked deed. How do I know? Well, take a look at me—stooped, matted coat, all flesh and bones. Driven out in the morning to find my own food. I can't even walk properly because of my limp. That's all the thanks I get after carrying my master safely on my back for nine years, bringing him into war and back and helping him transport his prisoners. Can you imagine that once I even had a saddle that glinted with jewels and three grooms to feed and look after me? Of course a kind deed is repaid by a wicked one."

Diassigue was nodding enthusiastically.

"Indeed, indeed. You couldn't have said a truer word," he shouted. Then he turned to Gone, who was looking very miserable, standing in the river up to his chest. "Time's up, Gone. I'm extraordinarily hungry."

"No!" shouted Gone. "That's not fair! You said three opinions."

Diassigue caught sight of Leuk the Hare hopping toward them.

"All right, all right. Here is your last chance," the crocodile replied.

When Leuk reached the bank, Diassigue called out, "Uncle Leuk, do you think you could share some of your wisdom with us? We need to know how should a good deed be rewarded—by a kind deed or a wicked deed?"

Leuk sat down.

"Hmmm," he murmured, rubbing his chin with his paw. "That's an interesting question and one that can't be answered until I ask you another. Would you ask a blind man to tell you if cotton is white or a crow is black?"

"Certainly not," replied Diassigue.

"I see. Well then, I can't possibly give you an answer until you tell me a bit more. What are these deeds you mention?"

Diassigue sighed. But seeing no other way, he began to relate the story:

"What happened was this: Gone found me in the bush. He rolled me in a mat and carried me here because I need a new home. I'm hungry—famished, actually—and if I don't eat soon I'll probably die. Gone would make a very good meal, and it would be stupid to let him go when I might not be able to find another one for days. And that's it, really," Diassigue finished.

"Well now," Leuk said, rubbing his chin again. "As far as I know, my ears are perfectly healthy so I must have heard every word you said. It seems to me, however, that several of your *words* are not healthy."

"Which ones do you mean?" cried Diassigue.

"The ones that said this child carried you in a mat from the bush to the river. I'm sorry, but I cannot believe that."

"But I really did," Gone put in. He wanted to be sure that Leuk understood all the details of the situation.

"I think not," said the hare. "I know how children like to make things up."

"But he really did," insisted Diassigue.

"Give me proof," said Leuk. "Come out of the water and show me how he did it."

Diassigue let go of Gone and they both climbed onto the bank.

"Show me," the hare commanded again, his whiskers twitching.

Diassigue crawled onto the mat. Gone rolled him up and tied the bundle with the lianas.

"What did you do then?" Leuk asked.

"I carried him on my head."

"Show me how you lifted him."

Gone heaved the dripping bundle onto his head.

"I see. Well, I need to know one more thing. Is this crocodile a special friend of your family?"

Gone shook his head.

"Then it's all right. Take this bundle home and have a good feast of crocodile meat tonight with all your friends and relations. That's how Diassigue should be repaid for forgetting your kind deed."

And that is exactly what happened.

# WHY THE MOON
# COMES OUT AT NIGHT

◆

A LONG TIME AGO, THE VAST KINGDOM OF THE sky was ruled by a powerful king. He had only two sons, Moon and Sun, and he married many wives in the hope of having more children. But the only wife who ever gave him children was the mother of Moon and Sun. She was a good mother, but she died when Sun, the younger boy, was still very small.

The king looked after his sons as best he could. But Sun clearly was his favorite, and so Moon learned early in life to be jealous of his younger brother. Behind their father's back, Moon was spiteful and mean, stealing Sun's playthings and grabbing the best morsels of food.

One day the king fell ill, and he knew that he would shortly die. He called his sons to his bedside and told them that he was dividing his kingdom into two equal parts, one for each of them. As Sun was still too young to rule, Moon was to look after Sun's lands until he came of age. The king also asked Moon to find Sun a good wife when the time came.

Moon promised his father he would take care of his brother, but soon afterward, the king died and Moon began to treat Sun very badly. When Sun said he wanted to raise sheep, cattle, or goats in preparation for someday offering a marriage dowry, Moon refused to give him any. And when Sun came of age and wanted to rule his own lands, Moon refused and threatened to kill his brother if he dared ask for anything else.

"I'm the oldest so I rule the whole kingdom. That's the way it should be and that's the way it's going to be," he roared.

Poor Sun realized that his life would be nothing but misery if he stayed in the kingdom of the sky, and so, without telling anyone, he left and traveled far, far away to a country that his father once had visited. Sun did not dare reveal his identity to anyone, for fear that his brother might find him. But disguised as a shepherd, he appeared before his father's friend, who was king of that land, and asked for work.

Now the king was a kind man. He had several daughters but no sons, and soon he treated Sun, who worked hard and was popular with all the household, like one of his own family. Sun shared their meals and joined their games. He liked all the princesses, but the youngest one was his particular favorite. She was full of fun and could make her sisters laugh with her imitations. But unfortunately for Sun, she was the king's favorite too, and one day he announced that she was to rule his kingdom after him and that her husband should come from one of the country's most important families.

Wealthy suitors arrived from all over the land, bringing lavish gifts. Soon there were so many that the line of young men stretched beyond the palace gates. The king decided that the only way to choose his daughter's husband was to set the men a task that would require enormous courage and skill.

Close to the palace was a large lake, and in the middle of this lake was an island of waving feathers that glinted with all the colors of the rainbow. People traveled for many days just to catch a glimpse of the magical feathers. The island was beautiful, but there was something sinister about it, too. Many men had tried to row out and retrieve some feathers, but each had mysteriously died in the attempt. Cattle, sheep, and goats grazing near the lake also had vanished from time to time.

In the past, the king asked several wise men for their opinions about the mystery. Some said there was undoubtedly a monster living in the lake that was protecting the feathers, and others thought that the feathers themselves had evil power.

So now the king set this task: The man who could bring back seven glinting feathers would win his daughter's hand.

Sun's liking for the king's daughter had changed to love, and, to his delight, she felt the same for him. Sun knew that without revealing his real identity, the only way to marry the princess was to retrieve the feathers.

Having heard all the stories, Sun looked long and hard at the lake and became convinced that some kind of water monster must be living in its depths. He devised a plan. The man-eating monster would easily hear a boat and could just as easily capsize it, but perhaps it could be surprised by a single underwater swimmer.

Sun wrapped coils of hollow lianas around a long stick. Then he went to the king and told him that he was going to try to fetch some of the feathers because he loved the princess very much and wanted to marry her. He asked the king if he could borrow the sharpest sword and the most piercing spear in

the palace. The king, though he could not accept the idea of his daughter marrying a shepherd, was willing to give Sun the weapons. Finally Sun went to one of the witch doctors for a poisonous potion, which he smeared on the tips of the sword and the spear.

The next morning, crowds of people gathered on the lakeshore to watch the first suitor's attempt. Sun looped the rope through a belt around his waist and put the end of it in his mouth. The king's daughter would stand on the shore and hold the other end, keeping it well clear of the water, so that Sun could breathe through the pipe while he swam. The rest of the rope was coiled up in a huge mound on the shore. Clutching his sword and spear in one hand, Sun waded into the lake. He turned to look at the king's daughter one last time, then dove in.

The rope uncoiled slowly and steadily as Sun swam farther and farther away. The princess held her end patiently, but as the hours went by and the rope still swished through her hands as it slipped into the water, her eyes filled with tears. When the king realized how unhappy his daughter was, he said, "Call your brave shepherd back. He doesn't need to prove himself any longer."

But the princess could not. If she pulled on the rope, it might fall out of Sun's mouth, and he might not have enough air to swim to the surface.

Toward the end of the day, when many in the crowd were beginning to think about going home, someone shouted, "Blood! Look out there, in the middle of the lake."

Sure enough, a huge red patch was spreading in the center of the lake. The crowd fell silent. When the princess saw the bloody pool, she fainted and fell to the ground. Her mother knelt down to help her while the king picked up the hollow rope and slowly shook it. To his amazement he could feel that there was still something attached to the other end.

Just as he was going to tell his daughter, there was a cry from the onlookers, and the king saw that some of the feathers were moving.

"It's coming to get us!" someone shouted.

"Run! Run! It's headed this way!" urged another.

But the king, who had lifted the rope up to his ear, roared, "SILENCE! The shepherd is still breathing."

By this time, the princess had recovered and she took the rope from her father and listened. A huge smile spread across her face as she realized that her shepherd was not only alive but swimming back toward shore.

Night had fallen and it was pitch black when Sun finally stepped out of the water, a raft of glorious, luminous feathers trailing behind him. A huge cheer went up from the crowd that had stayed to welcome him, and as the princess helped him out, the king banged his staff on the ground and spoke.

"This shepherd is the suitor worthy to be my daughter's husband."

It took Sun a few minutes to catch his breath, but then he thanked the king most graciously and made a long speech, explaining who he really was and why he had been forced to disguise himself. He then described how he had swum across the lake, surfaced just behind the head of the great monster, and stabbed it with the poisoned spear; how the monster had lashed its tail and how Sun could see that the feathers were attached to the monster's scaly body rather than to an island, as they had all thought; and how he slashed the beast's throat to make sure it was truly dead before slicing off its tail.

As he was finishing his story, there was a loud sloshing sound behind him, and all at once a long line of cows stepped out of the lake onto the shore. Behind them, several lines of goats emerged and, behind the goats, more than a hundred sheep. The people started to cheer and clap. The animals that had been swallowed alive by the monster were returning to their owners, alive and well.

There were great celebrations in the kingdom over the next few days. The king organized a magnificent wedding for his daughter, and Sun was given a large herd of cattle, goats, and sheep by all the people.

Sun wanted to return to the kingdom of the sky to see if he could persuade his brother to let him rule his own lands. So he set off with his new bride, several servants, and a large herd. But Moon had not changed in Sun's absence, and when he saw Sun's new wealth and radiant new bride, he was filled with jealousy. Sun had brought Moon many presents, including some of the magical feathers, so Moon had to appear to be grateful. He allowed Sun to build a house but he did not give his brother any land to rule.

But Sun was not concerned. He told his wife to be patient. He was sure he would win over his brother eventually.

One day Moon and Sun were walking by a salt clay mine. Moon asked Sun to dig some clay for the cattle while he went ahead to look for a cow that had strayed. When Sun was busy digging deep inside the mine, Moon returned and blocked up the entrance with slabs of clay.

Moon returned home and went to Sun's house. He told Sun's wife that her husband had been buried in a landslide at the mine. He said how sorry he was for her, but that he himself would look after her, as it was the custom in his kingdom that when a man died, his wife should marry his brother after a short period of mourning.

The princess was heartbroken and returned to her own country to tell her parents what had happened. Her mother tried to comfort her and said that she knew a witch doctor who had the skill to bring the dead back to life. Together they went to the witch doctor, who told the princess to find Sun's body, cut off some hair and a piece of his clothes, and put them in a clean calabash. She was then to hide the calabash in a safe place inside her house and to put small bits of meat into it every couple of days. At the end of two weeks, a small body would climb out of the calabash, identical to Sun's but in miniature. She must then feed the little man with delicious foods every day until he reached his normal size.

The princess went back to the kingdom of the sky and did exactly what the witch doctor had ordered. Everything happened just as he had said. But the princess was very nervous, for her time of mourning was nearly over. Would Sun be fully grown by the time of the wedding?

The princess's parents were invited to the wedding, and on the night before, they went to visit their daughter and spent quite a long time at her house.

The next morning, Moon looked extremely pleased with himself as the wedding guests arrived and presented their gifts. Everyone gathered in the palace and swapped news as they waited for Sun's wife to appear. Suddenly a loud voice could be heard above the din.

"Daughter," the visiting king cried. "Daughter, it is time to approach and show yourself to the people."

The princess walked into the palace, dressed in her usual clothes . . . and holding hands with Sun!

The king rushed up and embraced them both. The buzz of astonishment from the crowd was like the sound of ten thousand locusts. As the king explained to the people what really had happened between the brothers, Moon tried to slip away unnoticed. But the crowd caught him, and soon they were chanting, "Kill him! Kill him!"

Sun understood their anger, but he did not want to take revenge against his older brother. Instead, he suggested that Moon should be banished to a remote corner of the sky and allowed to move about only at night while the rest of the kingdom was asleep. Sun would rule over the whole of the sky during the day.

And that is exactly what happened.

# THE THUNDER-AND-
# LIGHTNING MONSTER

ONCE THERE WAS A WIDOW WHO LIVED WITH
her pretty daughter. Although the widow knew that her
daughter wanted to marry and have a family of her own, she
selfishly kept the girl at home.

"What would I do without you in the long, lonely evenings
and how would I manage the crops by myself?" she would
say. And so when suitors arrived with gifts, as they often did,
the widow said that her daughter was not interested in finding a husband and sent them away.

One day, when the girl went out to the fields to check on their rows of millet, she found that every single plant had been eaten right down to the ground.
All that was left were a few curly-edged stalks. She ran back and fetched her
mother. The widow was shocked at the sight of her ruined crop. Neither one
had any idea what sort of creature could have done such damage in just one
night. Luckily, a neighbor gave them some spare plants, and they spent the whole
day resetting the rows.

The next morning, they went out to check the new crop and found that over
half of the plants had been attacked and eaten right down to the ground. The
widow was very worried. She decided that the only thing to do was to build a
big fire at the edge of the field to scare away the animal that was destroying
their crop. As night fell, she herself lit the fire and sat down beside it to keep
watch. All she could hear was the crackling and sparking of the fire as she peered
into the darkness.

Suddenly she spotted a glowing light, as round as a gourd and as bright as
the full moon, at the far side of the field. She stood up and watched as the light

flickered on and off. Each time it seemed to be a little closer to her. Just then, a deep rumbling echoed across the fields, and the widow sat down, greatly relieved. It was only a thunderstorm, she told herself. But then a strange thing happened. The rumbling, thundering noise turned into a deep, loud voice, and she could clearly hear the words it spoke: "I cut the crop, I cut the crop, I shake the plants, I slash them down." Then the growling began again and the terrifying chant seemed to come from all sides. At the same time, the light no longer flickered on and off like lightning but began glowing continuously with an eerie brightness. As it came nearer and nearer, moving in a straight line, the widow knew for sure that it belonged to the animal that was destroying her even rows of millet plants.

Terrified that the creature would attack her next, the widow ran as fast as she could to her hut. She was so out of breath and trembling so violently that it took her several minutes to explain the terrible thunder-and-lightning monster to her daughter.

The next morning the widow went all through the village, telling her neighbors about the mysterious animal and offering a calabash of money to anyone who could kill it. During the following weeks, several men tried. But as soon as the rumbling voice thundered its chant across the fields, they all fled.

The widow was in a terrible state. The monster now had moved into her field of beans and was devouring that crop, too. The rainy season was nearly over, and with nothing to harvest, she and her daughter would have no food. In desperation, she asked her daughter to agree to marry any man who could kill the monster. The daughter agreed, and so the word went abroad that at last the girl was interested in finding a husband.

Now there was a young man in the village who had always admired the girl, but because he was very poor, he had no chance of offering her a dowry. As soon as he heard the news, he went straight to the widow and told her that if the girl would have him, he would go to the fields that night and kill the monster. The girl admired his courage and readily agreed to marry him if he was successful.

As night fell, the young man armed himself with a knife, sat by the fire, and waited for the monster to appear. When he saw the eerie light, he didn't close his eyes or turn his head. Instead he stood up and stared straight at it. But when the thundering voice began, he knew he wanted to run. He did not move, however, because he had decided that having the chance to marry the widow's daughter was worth the risk of being killed by the monster.

The voice grew so loud that he wanted to block his ears. But he held out his knife and stood his ground. The blinding light came nearer and nearer until it lit up the whole field. He could see his knife blade gleaming and his own hands trembling. Expecting at any moment to see a pair of bloodshot eyes and two vicious claws, the young man was astonished when he finally discerned at the heart of the light a small creature, shaped like a caterpillar, with an enormous glow shining around its tail. The thunder-and-lightning monster was nothing more than a glowworm.

The young man could hardly believe his luck. He tore off a piece of his shirt, caught the glowworm, and carefully wrapped it in the cloth. The dreadful thundering, which had scared so many grown men, finally stopped.

Now the suitor was so excited that he could not wait for dawn to break. He went straight to the widow's hut and told her he had caught the monster. In a flurry of excitement, she asked him to wait until morning. She wanted to call all the villagers together so that they could see the thunder-and-lightning monster for themselves.

When the people had gathered outside her hut, the boy unwrapped the piece of material he had been holding, and there was the tiny, harmless-looking glowworm.

There were shrieks of laughter from the crowd. Then some shouted, "Go home and stop wasting our time," and "Couldn't you find something a little bit bigger?" But just then, the young man touched the glowworm's tail, and it emitted a blinding flash of light. The crowd fell silent. The next moment, the glowworm sang its thundering chant so loudly that many of the people jumped with fear.

Nobody understood how the glowworm could make such a terrifying noise and how its glow could be quite so blinding. But the villagers had to admit the young man was the only person brave enough to face the monster and that he deserved to marry the widow's daughter. The widow kept her promise, and the two young people were happily married just a few weeks later.

# THE POOR MAN'S REWARD

◈

ONCE THERE WAS A YOUNG MAN WHO WAS very poor. Since his parents had died when he was only a boy, he had been brought up by his grandparents. But now they were dead, too, and he was lonely and unhappy. He had no cattle, no fine clothes, and no valuable belongings, and because of this the people of his village ignored him.

One day the poor man decided to leave the unfriendly village. He would travel to another part of the country—it didn't matter where—and see if he could find better luck.

The young man packed all the food he had, which was a small amount of meat, a thin sack of millet, and some honey, and he filled a large gourd with water. Very early the next morning, before anyone else awoke, he set off toward the east.

The man walked for miles across the dusty plain and by the middle of the day had grown hot and tired. Luckily there was a tree nearby, so he sat and rested in its shade. Feeling hungry, he opened his bag and took out the millet, which was wrapped in a cloth. Just then he heard a voice above him.

"I'm starving. Please may I have some of your millet?"

He looked up and saw a weaverbird perched on a branch above him. It looked thin and bedraggled. Astonished that the bird could talk, the man replied, "Of course you can," and stretched up his arms with the sack so that the bird could peck at the grain. There was only a little bit left at the bottom when the bird had finished.

"Thank you," said the weaverbird. "I won't forget your kindness."

The man ate the rest of the millet and went on his way. He walked until dark

and then climbed into a tree to sleep. In the morning he set off again, and at midday once more he sat down in the shade of a tree to shelter himself from the burning sun. This time he thought he would eat the meat. Just as he was pulling off a chunk, he heard something scratching the ground behind him. He looked around and there was a scrawny-looking hyena, eyeing him nervously.

"Excuse me," it said, "but do you think you could spare the bones when you've finished the meat? I haven't eaten for two days and I'm feeling faint."

The man could hardly believe his eyes. Here was a hyena, standing next to him and speaking very politely. He could see drops of saliva forming at the edge of the hyena's mouth and realized that it was ravenously hungry. He decided once again to share his meal.

"Hold on a minute. I'll just take a mouthful or two and then you can have the rest."

The hyena crouched patiently beside the man, and in no time at all a bone, with plenty of meat still attached, was placed by its front paws. The hyena ripped off the meat and swallowed it in a few gulps, then settled down to gnaw the bone. The man stood up to go.

"Oh!" said the hyena. "I enjoyed my meal so much I nearly forgot to say thank you. But I won't forget your kindness."

The man trekked on, his feet sore and his face burning from the heat of the sun. At dusk he found a tree to sleep in and the following morning he started out early, with only some honey and the gourd of water left in his bag.

At midday his legs were aching and he sat down to rest by some bushes. He took out the small gourd of honey, dipped his fingers in, and began to eat. As the delicious sweetness slid down his throat, he felt much better. He was just taking another mouthful when he heard a buzzing near his ear. Then a tiny voice said, "I'd love some of that. There isn't any nectar for miles."

It was a bee. By this time, the man wasn't surprised to hear a talking animal. He felt sorry for the hungry creature and immediately held out the gourd. The bee had a good feed, then flew up to the man's head and whispered, "Thank you, sir. I won't forget your kindness."

Later that afternoon, feeling dry and dusty, the man stopped to have a drink. Just as he lifted the large gourd to his lips, he heard a deep, husky voice coming from the grasses behind him.

"Water. Just a sip. Parched."

The man turned around and jumped backward when he saw an enormous, mud-caked crocodile, its tongue hanging out between its long, fearsome teeth.

"Lost my way. No water. Need drink. Now."

Not very polite, thought the man, but the crocodile certainly had lost its way and did look very dry. Nervously the man walked up to the gaping jaws and held out the gourd.

"Open wide," he said. "I'll give you a drink."

He poured most of the contents of the gourd into the huge mouth. The crocodile gulped noisily.

"Thanks," it rasped. "Won't forget your kindness."

Then it slowly crawled away, its tongue no longer lolling out.

As the man walked along, he thought to himself that his luck certainly had not changed yet. He had no food left, barely a dribble of water, and there was no town or settlement in sight.

Just then he spied another man on the side of a hill and hurried toward that spot. The stranger waited for him, greeting him in a friendly way, and the two began to talk. The young man discovered that he was in a part of the country that belonged to a very wealthy king. In fact, the king's palace was just on the other side of the hill. The stranger suggested that the young man should go there without delay, because the king was offering his daughter and his kingdom to any man who could pick out the princess from a crowd of people. It wasn't as easy as it sounded, he explained, because the princess had been brought up with several other girls in a distant palace, and no one had ever seen her before.

The man thanked the stranger and toiled up the hill. When he reached the

top, he looked down and saw below him a large village with a magnificent palace at one end of it. As he reached the outskirts of the village, he could hear the babble of many voices, and when he made his way to the meeting place, he found that it already was packed with people. More strangers, like himself, were arriving and joining the crowd every few minutes.

There seemed to be a wall of faces in front of him. How was he going to be able to move around and see all the young girls? What would a princess look like? When he looked down at his own dusty, shabby clothes, he felt disheartened. Even if he did pick out the princess, she certainly would not accept him.

People everywhere were shouting with excitement, and the young man felt hot and bothered. On top of everything, an insect was buzzing around his head and would not go away. But suddenly he heard a tiny, familiar voice.

"Don't worry," whispered the voice. "It's only me, the bee you helped a few days ago. Now it's my turn to help you. Stand on that bank over there and watch me. I'll fly to a girl and pretend to sting her. She'll probably throw her arms in the air and try to brush me away. Once you've seen her, I'll fly off. Go and claim her then—she will be the king's daughter."

Before the young man had time to thank the bee, it flew back into the crowd. So he did as the bee suggested and climbed up onto the grassy bank. He had completely lost sight of his friend, but in a moment the young man saw a girl frantically waving her arms in the air. He made straight for her, and as he came near, she stopped waving. Now he could see that she was very beautiful. He hesitated at first, but then went up to her and said, "You are the king's daughter."

The girl nodded and word went through the crowd that she had been claimed. The king came up, but when he saw how poor the young man was, he suddenly said, "Yes, yes, this is my daughter, but of course you realize that's not all you have to do to win her. There are many other tasks, and you must complete them all before you can marry."

Then the king announced the second task: The man was to sort a heap of mixed seeds into separate piles of millet, maize, and sorghum. When the king showed the poor man the size of the heap—a hill of seeds that filled nearly half the courtyard—and told him that the task was to be finished by the next morning, the man shook his head in silence. How could he possibly do it in just one night?

He was sitting down, with his head between his hands, when a small bird alighted on his shoulder.

"Hello, friend," it said. "Can I be of any help?"

The man was delighted to see the weaverbird again and explained his problem. The bird cocked its head on one side for a minute and then chirped, "I'll be right back. Don't go away."

The man sat patiently, wondering what the little bird would do. Then he saw what looked like a gray cloud moving toward him above the palace roof. As the swirling cloud rolled closer, he could make out the wings of hundreds of weaverbirds, all heading for the courtyard. They landed on the ground, and before the man had time to realize what was happening, they delved into the pile and picked up the seeds, one by one, and carried them in their beaks to the other side of the courtyard.

"We're good at this sort of thing," explained the friendly weaverbird as the man watched the three new piles growing steadily and the original hill shrinking. Before the first cock started to crow, the birds had finished, and they flew off in a flock over the palace roof. The man shouted "Thank you!" after them.

When the king's servants arrived at daybreak, the man was standing, grinning, in front of the piles. The guards reported the scene to the king, who rushed into the courtyard and stared at the unexpected sight.

"Indeed," he muttered. "Yes...yes...well, of course, that's only the second task. There will be another this evening."

The king hurried from the courtyard, and the man wondered what might be in store for him next. Later that day he saw the servants killing a bull and boiling it in a huge pot. When he went to the palace in the evening, the king told him that his task for the night was to eat all of the meat of the cooked bull, right down to the bones.

Now here was a task he could handle, thought the man. When he took his first few mouthfuls, he was ravenous, remembering all his days of near starvation. But soon he felt stuffed and could not eat another bite. Yet a mountain of meat remained on the ground in front of him. All of a sudden, he spotted the bright eyes of an animal creeping toward the carcass. It was a hyena. The man looked around to see where he could hide when he heard a voice.

"Don't be frightened, kind sir, it's only me, the hyena you fed out on the plains. What are you doing here?"

As the man explained his impossible task, a big smile spread across the hyena's face.

"Allow me to make a suggestion," it said, when the man had finished. "Let me fetch my family and we will have no trouble dealing with this little problem of yours. Just you wait and see."

The hyena disappeared but returned in just a few minutes with several hungry-looking hyenas. They wasted no time at all. Positioning themselves all around the carcass, they tore off every bit of meat until all that was left was a pile of bones. The man couldn't believe his luck: three impossible tasks and he had achieved them all, thanks to the animals.

The next morning, the astonished and desperate king announced the last task of all. Confident that this task would be truly impossible, he stood in the meeting place and addressed his people.

"On the other side of our wide river there is a magical ostrich feather. This man must cross the river in broad daylight and return with the feather. Then he may marry my daughter and become king when I die."

The gathered people fell silent for a moment and then walked in a body down to the water. When the man stood on the bank, he realized what the crowd already knew. Breaking the surface of the muddy water were the bulging eyes and lashing tails of hundreds of crocodiles. It was a terrifying sight.

All of a sudden, the young man felt as if his feet were bolted to the ground. He could not move. If he went forward, he certainly would be killed. If he went backward, he would lose the king's daughter, who was standing on the bank and looking at him admiringly. A deep voice interrupted his thoughts.

"Here. At your feet. Need something?"

There was the crocodile he had helped, looking much happier than before. Delighted, the man explained his problem.

"Problem?" said the crocodile. "No problem. You'll see. Kind man." And with a swish of his tail, the crocodile disappeared underwater.

The man stared at the river as the crocodiles gathered together with much splashing and thrashing in the direct center. Then, as if they'd been given an order, they formed a straight line that stretched from bank to bank, each crocodile holding the tail of the next in his teeth.

"Step across," said the man's friend, who was once more at his feet. "Bridge of crocodiles."

As the man stepped onto the crocodiles' backs the crowd started to clap and shout. Even the king was impressed. The man was so excited he walked faster and faster over the living bridge until he reached the other side. He picked up the ostrich feather sticking out of the ground and ran back across the crocodiles' backs. When he stepped off, he turned and thanked his crocodile friend.

"Anytime," replied the crocodile, and it sank back under the water until only its huge eyes could be seen. The people crowd-ed around to congratulate the successful suit-or as he made his way through the crowd to the king and his daughter.

"There's no doubt about it, you're a remarkable young man," said the king. "Wel-come to my family."

The princess smiled in agreement, and the young man knew that his lonely days were gone forever.

# WACU AND THE EAGLE

◆

THERE ONCE WAS A PRETTY KIKUYU GIRL named Wacu who was an only child. Her father was a very rich man. He had a big herd of cattle, over a hundred sheep, and many goats. Wacu loved to help him in the fields during the day and at milking time in the evening. She loved her mother too, but she wasn't at all interested in helping around the house, like the other girls in her village. When Wacu was not herding animals, she joined the boys in their wrestling matches and long-jump contests. In fact, she was so good at boys' games that she often won.

As time went by, Wacu's father began to treat her as a son. In the evenings he would let her come into his *thingira*,* to share his meal of meat and milk and to hear his stories. The Kikuyu custom was that boys and men could eat meat in public, but girls and women were only allowed to eat it in their homes, and then only on religious feast days.

When Wacu was old enough to become a woman, she joined the other girls in a coming-of-age ceremony. After this, she was expected to do women's household chores and to prepare herself for becoming a wife. But word had spread that Wacu was a meat-eater. Most of the young men did not want a meat-eating wife, and so they ignored Wacu even though she was pretty and very hard-working.

After a while, Wacu grew tired of waiting for someone to propose to her. She enjoyed her meals of meat, and if marriage meant giving them up, she would not bother with it. She slipped out into the fields and began to herd her father's animals again. Whenever she felt like a good meal of juicy meat, she slaughtered a sheep and ate it.

*thingira: a hut where fathers and sons gather in the Kikuyu tradition

One day she went to visit a cousin who lived in the hill country, three days' walk from her village. She accompanied her cousin to many dances, and one night she met a good-looking young man who danced with her all evening. They met again the next day, and the next, and by the end of the week, Wacu realized that she was in love. She was surprised and delighted when the young man asked her to marry him.

Wacu's parents were very excited about the proposal and told her how wonderful it was that she had found a young man who wanted to marry her. They warned her that of course she must give up her habit of eating meat. Wacu agreed with them and told herself she would not mind doing without meat.

The wedding was arranged, and the dowry was paid. Wacu and the young man were married.

For a few weeks, Wacu found that she could easily do without meat. But after watching her husband kill and roast several sheep and smelling the delicious aromas of the juices that wafted up from the fire, Wacu felt hunger pangs for meat again. Why shouldn't she be able to eat it? She wasn't harming anyone and it wasn't harming her.

So Wacu decided to buy meat in the marketplace and cook and eat it when her husband was out. This went on for several years. Meanwhile, Wacu had three sons and was very happy as a wife and mother.

One day Wacu decided she was tired of eating meat in secret. She brought home a joint of meat and cooked it right in front of her husband. He was shocked. His wife was a meat-eater and he had never known a thing about it. When he angrily told her never to eat meat again, Wacu said that she had been doing so all her life and that she enjoyed it, just as he did. Why should she stop now?

Wacu's husband realized that he

would not be able to persuade her to stop eating meat, so he began to hide the housekeeping money. And when he killed a lamb for himself and his male relatives, he refused to give any to his wife, not even a taste, not even on a feast day. But neither of these tricks worked, because Wacu would set up such a wail and curse him with such a piercing cry that he had to put his hands over his ears. Even so, he could still hear the awful words of the curse, which he knew had the power to bring bad luck on his house. To keep away the evil spirits, he would kill another lamb and offer his wife some meat. And so Wacu continued to get her way.

Wacu's husband was in a terrible state. Wacu was a good wife and he and their sons loved her very much. He didn't want her to have to return to her father's house after such a long time. But she was making a fool of him, eating meat for all to see and telling the neighbors that preventing women from sharing such delicious food was a silly custom. Soon the whole village was talking about her unusual habits.

One day the elders held a meeting in the fields. As usual, all the menfolk of the village went, and the younger men killed and roasted several goats and lambs. The elders started to speak about the problem of Wacu. One of them banged his staff on the ground and declared that he knew Wacu was a hard-working wife and mother and that perhaps she was right. Perhaps women should be allowed to share meat with their husbands. Another elder agreed, pointing out that Masai women ate meat without any problems. But other elders disagreed strongly. They said a Kikuyu custom, passed down by their forefathers, should not be flouted. There was no reason to change the custom now, just because one man was having difficulty with his wife. The meat-eating Wacu should be sent back to her father.

As the elders' discussion grew more and more heated and the sound of their arguments drifted across the hills, the young men had finished cooking the meat and were laying it on banana leaves to cool. Suddenly a huge, dark shadow appeared in the sky. As it drew closer the men could discern the shape of an eagle. But here was no ordinary eagle; its curved beak and grasping claws were twice the normal size, and its staring eyes were a deep, fathomless purple. The men ran for their lives as the great bird dropped down from the sky.

To everyone's surprise, the eagle ignored them all. It landed on the ground and, curling its vast claws around the carcasses, picked up the cooked meat and flew effortlessly toward the distant hills.

When the men realized that they were safe, they came out of their hiding places. Some of the younger ones began to run after the eagle, certain that it would drop some of its load. They sprinted up the first hill and down into a valley that stretched far into the distance. At the very horizon, they thought they could see the eagle landing and so kept up their pace until they reached the end of the valley.

The eagle had landed on a field. To the men's amazement, it was dropping all the meat in front of a young woman who had been weeding. Then it stretched its powerful wings and took off, flying toward the forest of Kiri-Nyaga and the sacred mountain of Nyaga. By the time the men reached the woman, she was sitting on the ground, chewing noisily at a leg of lamb as the juices dribbled from the sides of her mouth. The men looked at one another in silence. Of course this was Wacu, they realized. They didn't dare snatch the carcasses away, because the eagle had deliberately offered them to her. Instead the astonished warriors raced back to the elders and told them what they had witnessed.

The elders insisted on seeing this extraordinary sight for themselves and walked over the hill and into the valley until they came to Wacu's field. When they saw her enjoying her meal of roasted meat, the carcasses piled high in front of her like an offering, they decided that the eagle must have been a messenger from God, showing them that it was right for women to eat meat. They agreed that from that day on, all Kikuyu women should be allowed to eat meat in their homes with their menfolk.

# HOW THE WILD TURKEY
# GOT ITS SPOTS

LONG AGO NGANGA, THE WILD TURKEY, WAS AS black as night. Lion, the king of the jungle, did not trust her one bit because she was a clever bird and always up to tricks.

One day Lion was hungry and decided that he would like a good feed of beef. He spotted a cow whose back was turned to him. This cow already was known for fighting off big animals with her huge, pointed horns. So Lion broke into a run and charged right up behind her. He was just about to sink his teeth into her shoulder and pull her to the ground when a thick cloud of dust blew up in his face. He coughed and spluttered as the dust choked him. Then he let out a mighty roar as pieces of grit burned his eyes. For several minutes, Lion could not see a thing.

When the dust settled, he caught sight of Nganga's tail feathers as she scuttled away into the scrub. The dust cloud must have been her mischief.

Lion was furious. Not only had Nganga interrupted his kill, she also had created so much dust that it covered the cow's footprints. Lion could not even chase after his prey. Nganga was nothing but trouble.

A few days later, Lion's cheered up when he spied the cow walking down to the stream for a drink. Now he would get his beef! He crept up on her, but the cow must have heard him coming because she turned just in time and lowered her horns. Lion leapt at her, aiming for her side, when suddenly he was covered in yet another cloud of dust. Choking, he fell to the ground, his eyes watering and stinging. This time he could hear Nganga as she puffed and blew, forcing the dust up into a whirling cloud.

When at last Lion's vision was clear, the cow once more had disappeared and Nganga was flying off toward the trees.

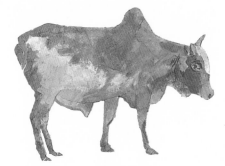

Lion had had enough. Nganga had spoiled his hunting too many times. He would have to get rid of her. He found out where she kept her chicks and lay in wait. After a while Nganga appeared, with several of her children running behind her. Lion sprang out from his hiding place, but Nganga was too quick for him and flew up in the air. Then she attacked him from above, pecking his back with her sharp beak. Lion roared as the chicks screamed and ran for cover and Nganga kept up her attack. But it was hard work, keeping away from Lion's snarling jaws, and soon she had to fly down to the water for a quick drink.

There, on the bank, Nganga saw the cow with the pointed horns.

"Quick," whispered the cow. "Over here. Let me help you."

Nganga ran over. The cow wet the tip of her tail with her own milk and swished it back and forth, all over Nganga's body, sprinkling her black feathers with little white dots. Then the cow hid behind a bush. Just then Lion limped up to Nganga, who was now a striking, black-and-white spotted bird.

"Have you seen Nganga, by any chance?" he asked.

Nganga disguised her voice and said, "Yes, she went that way a few minutes ago. She was heading for the forest."

Lion limped off toward the forest, and the cow came out of hiding.

"What a clever trick!" giggled Nganga. "I couldn't have done better myself. Thank you, my friend, for saving my life."

"A pleasure, dear Nganga. And thank you for saving mine."

Then the cow told Nganga to bring her chicks to be sprinkled with milk too, in case Lion returned.

And that is how the wild turkey got its spots.

# THE TRAVELERS' FRIEND

◈

 THERE ONCE WAS A MAN WHO WAS COMING home after being away on business for several weeks. He was tired and hungry; the journey had taken longer than he expected, and his food and water had run out several days before. Now he was finishing his walk across an especially dry and dusty part of the countryside, and he was delighted to see in the distance the rocky cliffs, the trees and grasses of his green homelands. He also was relieved that he had made it through the desert safely because other travelers from his neighborhood had disappeared without a trace on that stretch of land.

The first tree he came to was growing right in front of a great slab of rock. He decided to rest in its shade for a while before beginning the last leg of his journey. As he sat down he felt something wet dripping onto his arm. Straightaway he rummaged in his bag and pulled out his drinking bowl. What luck to find a tree with a water vine, he thought.

He held up his bowl and filled it quickly, but just as he was about to drink, a dove flew out of nowhere and with a flurry of its wings knocked the bowl from his hands. All the water spilled out. The man was annoyed. But since the dove had flown up into the tree, there was not much he could do. He picked up his bowl and once more began to fill it.

When the bowl was full, the man grasped it tightly and lifted it to his lips, when *swoosh!* The bird knocked it away again. This time the man batted out with his hand at the interfering dove. But the bird was too quick for him and flew up once more into the safety of the tree.

The man's temper was rising. His mouth was now uncomfortably dry and the wretched bird was preventing him from getting a drink.

Determined that he was not going to be deprived of water, the man tried again. This time he waited for the fluttering wings to come, and right before they reached him, he pulled back his arm and flung the bowl at the dove. It hit the bird so hard that the little feathered body fell to the ground like a coconut.

Good, thought the man. Now I can get a drink in peace.

But just then he heard a faint noise coming from the tiny creature at his feet. He looked down and saw that the dove was still breathing, although it lay motionless. Then it tried to lift its head. The bird was looking at a spot halfway up the tree, just above where the man was standing. The man suddenly realized that the dove was trying to tell him something. He looked up, and to his horror, he saw a yellow-eyed snake as big as a man, its head resting on a branch. The "water" he had been about to drink was in fact poison, dripping from the serpent's opened fangs.

The man glanced back down at the dove, but by now it was dead. With a shudder, he turned and ran like the wind toward his home. As the man sped across the fields, all he could think about was how he had mistreated the dove. He was deeply ashamed of having lost his temper.

When the traveler arrived home, he told all the men in his village what had happened. They agreed that the dove must have seen the wily snake tricking and then eating other travelers. It had probably tried but failed to warn their neighbors who had disappeared so mysteriously on that stretch of the journey.

The man suggested that they should kill the snake straightaway. So they filled the carcass of a goat with poison and dragged it across the land, back to where the snake lay hidden. They waited till dark, carried the carcass to the tree, and watched from behind the rocks. At dawn, the snake slid down the trunk and gorged itself on the poisoned goat. The men did not even have to wait for the poison to take effect—the snake was so fat and heavy that it could not slither back up the tree trunk. They attacked it from all sides, hacking it to pieces with their swords. Then they built a huge fire and threw the bits into the flames.

Thanks to the dove, from that day on travelers were once more able to cross the dry land in safety.

# WHY HYENAS DON'T WEAR JEWELRY

THE WIVES OF BOUKI THE HYENA AND LEUK the Hare were rather plain-looking. They were extremely sensitive about this, and whenever they heard the word *ugly*, they presumed the speaker was talking about them.

"We must find some way of making ourselves look pretty," said Leuk's wife one day.

"Maybe if we had some brightly colored jewelry—beaded necklaces, bracelets, anklets, and belts," suggested Bouki's wife.

Leuk's wife thought that was a good idea, and they both decided to ask their husbands to find them some jewels.

Bouki and Leuk agreed and set off in different directions to look for jewelry. Bouki, who wanted to get the job done as quickly as possible, stopped at the first marshy place he came to and dug up some wet clay. He shaped it into many balls of different sizes and poked a thorn through each one to make a hole. Then he left them on a rock to dry in the sun while he crawled under a bush to take a nap. Later that day, he strung the balls together with dried plant stems until he had made several necklaces, bracelets, anklets, and belts. Then he returned home.

When his wife saw the jewelry, she was very pleased. It wasn't quite as colorful as she had hoped, but at least she would look better than all the other hyena wives.

Meanwhile Leuk had been searching everywhere, scampering up steep hills, through thorny thickets, and across dusty grasslands. He'd been away from home for several days and still hadn't found any jewels for his wife. Exhausted, he was glad to rest for a short while at the foot of a huge baobab tree.

"Ah! That's better," he sighed as he stretched out on the ground.

Suddenly he heard a voice from above him. "Good sir, if you'd like to try something pleasurable, taste my leaves."

Leuk looked up and realized that the tree was speaking to him. He stood up, picked three leaves, and ate them.

"*Mmmmm.* Delicious. Thank you!"

"Why not try some of my fruit too? It's even tastier," said the tree.

Leuk scrambled up the thick trunk of the baobab and picked one of the long, club-shaped fruit that all the animals called monkey bread because only Golo the Monkey knew how to pick and eat it. Leuk carried the fruit down to the ground and followed the tree's instructions. He split open the shell and bit into the juicy pulp.

"My goodness! What a flavor! If only I could get a supply of these, I could set up a fruit business and grow rich."

"Is it riches you're interested in?" asked the baobab.

Leuk nodded.

"Then climb my trunk again and look into the crack halfway up."

Leuk scrambled up once more, pressed his face close to the trunk, and peered through the crack. When he saw what was inside he nearly fell off the trunk in astonishment. The hollow trunk was packed full of jewels and pieces of beautiful cloth that sparkled and glinted in the dark. He clung on tight to the tree with his back paws and tried to poke his front paws through the slit.

"Hold on a minute," said the baobab. "Those treasures don't belong to me, so I can't give them to you. But if you go into the gombo fields over there, you'll find someone who can."

Leuk was very excited. He had never seen so many jewels in all his life. He could just imagine his wife's happiness when he gave them to her.

He thanked the baobab tree and hurried over to the fields, where rows of gombo plants were growing. Standing in the middle of one field was a small goblin with hair down to his thighs. He was tossing stones into the air and catching them again, and he jumped with fright when Leuk called to him.

"Don't worry, Kouss," said Leuk. "I'm not going to hurt you. Gouye the Baobab told me to come here because—"

"Kouss knows. Kouss knows. Leuk comes with Kouss. Kouss shows Leuk hole in tamarind tree where Kouss lives. When Father Kouss comes home, he tries to put club against fence. But club picks Father up and tosses him over fence. Leuk must not laugh. When Mother Kouss comes home with bundle of sticks on head, sticks pick her up and toss her onto ground. Leuk must not laugh. Mother kills chicken and cooks for Leuk. But Mother gives Leuk roasted feathers and throws away meat. Leuk must eat feathers. Leuk must not show surprise."

With that, Kouss started to hop to the edge of the field. Leuk practiced not looking surprised as he followed the hopping goblin along a path to a large tamarind tree. He climbed into the hollow trunk after Kouss and waited until evening. Sure enough, everything happened exactly as the young goblin had predicted. Leuk did not look surprised; he did not laugh, and he pretended that it was quite normal to eat roasted feathers, even though he almost choked on the spiky spines and had to spit them out when Mother Kouss was not looking.

Leuk spent three days inside the tamarind with Kouss's family. On the fourth day, Kouss said, "Father Kouss comes home tonight. Offers Leuk two calabashes. Leuk must take small calabash."

Leuk didn't ask Kouss any questions. He just waited until the father returned that evening and offered him two calabashes, just as Kouss had predicted. Leuk chose the smaller one. Then Kouss said, "Leuk goes home now. In hut, alone, Leuk says to calabash, 'Keul, keep your promise.' Leuk sees what happens."

Bursting with excitement, Leuk thanked the goblins for all their hospitality, climbed down the tree, and bounded home. There was no one there, so he shut

himself into his hut and put the calabash on the floor. As soon as he could say, "Keul, keep your promise," sparkling jewels and lengths of fine cloth in every shade of blue from indigo to aquamarine filled the calabash until they reached the rim and spilled onto the floor. Leuk jumped up and down with delight.

When Leuk's wife returned and saw the jewelry, she jumped even higher than Leuk had.

"Oh, Leuk, you are the best husband ever," she cried.

The next day Leuk's wife decorated herself with bracelets, necklaces, anklets, and a belt and tied a shimmering piece of blue cloth around her waist. Then, carrying a calabash on her head, she set off for the well.

She was filling her calabash with water when along came Bouki's wife, wearing her new clay jewelry. When Bouki's wife saw Leuk's wife, she stopped in her tracks and opened her mouth as if to speak. But her mouth stayed open and no sound came out. Then suddenly she keeled over and lay on her back, her feet sticking up in the air like four sticks, and her beads scattered all over the ground.

Leuk's wife thought her hyena friend was acting foolishly and shouted at her to get up. Bouki's wife did not stir, and when Leuk's wife put down her calabash and went over, she saw that the hyena had fainted.

She fetched her calabash, ran back from the well, and poured water on her friend's face.

"You...I...," the hyena spluttered as she picked herself up and stared at the hare's jewels closely. Then she turned her back and staggered toward her home, her wet fur leaving puddles behind her. When she reached the hut, Bouki was just waking up and stretching.

"Get up, you lazy good-for-nothing hyena!" screeched Bouki's wife. "Leuk's wife is dripping with gold and silver and pearls and rubies and emeralds. If you don't get me a set of jewelry that's just as gorgeous as hers, I'm going back to my father."

Bouki slunk out of the hut without a word and spent the day searching high and low for some proper jewels. In the evening, he hit upon a plan. He took a handful of monkey nuts and chewed them into a pulp. Then he packed the pulp between his cheek and gum on one side of his mouth and went off to find Leuk.

"*Uuuuuuu,*" he moaned, when he saw the hare.

"What's the matter, Bouki?" asked Leuk.

"Oh, Leuk, I have a terrible toothache. Put me out of my misery and pull out my tooth."

"Well, I'd like to help, Bouki, but I'm thinking about how close my paw would be to your sharp teeth."

"How could I bite you, my friend, when I haven't even the strength to sip a mouthful of water?"

"Oh, all right. Open your mouth and show me which tooth it is."

Bouki quickly swallowed the nut pulp and opened his mouth wide, pointing to his left side. Leuk touched the teeth one by one, saying, "Is it this one?" Bouki shook his head each time. But when Leuk touched the back tooth, Bouki snapped his jaws shut and sunk his teeth into Leuk's paw.

Leuk yelped in pain.

"You can shout all you like," said Bouki through his clenched teeth, "but I won't let you go until you tell me where you got all those jewels."

"I'll tell you when the first cock crows tomorrow."

"Promise?"

"I swear on my father's belt."

Bouki released Leuk and they both went home.

Very early next morning, when the air was still cold, Bouki got up. He was so impatient to find the jewels that he went out to his own rooster and poked it until it started to crow. Then he ran to Leuk's hut and shouted, "Get up! Get up! The first cock has crowed."

Leuk came out, and seeing that it was still cold and dark, he guessed that Bouki must have played a trick on him.

"All right, I heard it, but the old folks haven't started to cough yet. When I hear them coughing, I'll know that the day is really beginning."

Bouki disappeared, and a few minutes later Leuk heard the familiar early-morning noises of the village elders as they started to stir. Leuk realized that there was no point in delaying any longer—Bouki would only think up some other trick. So he led the hyena to the baobab tree and on the way there explained to him what he should do and say.

When Leuk had gone, Bouki sat down to wait for the tree to speak. But suddenly he leapt up, as if he had been attacked by ants, and started to pace around the trunk. After circling it seven times he stopped and spoke.

"Gouye, I'm Bouki. I've heard that your shade is cool, your leaves are tasty, and your fruit is delicious. But I'm a busy fellow and I haven't got time to wait here until the sun gets hot or my stomach begins to rumble with hunger. I know about the riches in your trunk so just tell me where I can find the Kouss who can provide me with jewels like yours. Then I'll be off."

The baobab directed him to the gombo fields. Bouki waited there impatiently until midday. At last he spotted the goblin. He went up to him and pinioned the creature's feet under his heavy paws.

"Little Kouss, have you seen any fine jewels recently?"

The goblin flinched as Bouki cuffed his ears.

"I'm sure you'd like to share some with poor old Bouki."

The terrified goblin tried to escape as Bouki kept hitting him.

"Kouss and Bouki could be the best of friends if Little Kouss is prepared to share some of his treasures. Now don't you think that's a good idea?"

By this time, the goblin was nodding enthusiastically. He would have agreed to anything to make Bouki stop.

Bouki let him go and the goblin gave him the same instructions as he had given Leuk. Then he led Bouki to the tamarind tree and they climbed in.

Like Leuk, Bouki stayed three days with the goblins, but he behaved very differently. He scoffed and laughed at every strange thing that happened. On the fourth day, when it came to choosing between the two calabashes, the young goblin decided not to tell Bouki which calabash to choose. Although Bouki actually remembered Leuk's advice, he ignored it, saying to himself, What a fool I'd be to choose the smaller calabash when there's bound to be more jewels in the bigger one.

As soon as he'd made his choice, Bouki grabbed the calabash and started to scramble out of the tree. Father Kouss shouted down to him, "When you get home, you must say to the calabash, 'Keul, keep your promise.'"

Bouki didn't even bother to thank him but ran straight home. He dragged a huge tree trunk against the gate of the kraal. Then he told his wife, who was pounding millet outside, to pile cooking pots, pestles, and mortars and anything else she could find against the door of his hut once he'd gone inside.

"I'm about to provide you with some magnificent jewels. Don't let anyone in until I say so," he shouted through his barricaded door.

Bouki's wife could see that he wasn't going to say any more about where he'd been or what he was going to do inside the hut. So she did what he asked and then returned to her millet.

Bouki put the calabash on the floor, took a deep breath, and said, "Keul, keep your promise."

Immediately a huge stick, almost as thick as a fence pole, shot out of the calabash and started to beat Bouki around the ears with all the force of a giant. As Bouki screamed and ducked, the stick moved down his body, hitting him all over. Bouki hurled himself against the door of his hut with such force that he broke it down. He flew outside, still dodging to escape the blows, and there was a terrible clatter as he tripped over all the pots and other cooking utensils. He had to stop at the outside gate to heave at the tree trunk. Finally, he was able to squeeze through to the path, and his wife watched in amazement as he ran into the bush faster than he ever had run before, chased by the stick.

Bouki did not return for several days, and when he did he was covered with bruises and was limping badly. There was no mention of jewels and his wife never asked for any again. In fact, hyenas have never bothered with jewelry or fine cloth to this day.

# WHY HYENAS
# DON'T RUN ERRANDS

EVERYONE AGREED THAT PENDA WAS THE MOST beautiful girl in the village of M'Badane. Even so, Penda wasn't happy; she had already turned sixteen and was still not married. Most of her friends had at least one baby tied onto their backs by now.

If it had been up to her, Penda would have had no trouble choosing a husband. There were plenty of young men available. Almost every day, messengers arrived from other villages with presents and proposals of marriage from their masters. Some brought jewelry, some cattle, some food; others brought fine clothes. But they were all turned away, for it was up to Mor, Penda's father, to choose her a husband, and he was not interested in the usual gifts, be they from peasants, rich merchants, or even holy men. Instead, Mor set the suitors a strange task: Whoever could kill an ox and deliver the meat to Mor by hyena would win Penda as his wife. However, not even one mouthful of the meat could be missing.

The suitors all complained loudly about the unfairness of the task. How could you give meat to a hyena and expect the beast not to touch it? You might as well try to forbid the thirsty sand from drinking the first rain after months of drought. You might as well give a child a calabash of honey and expect him not to dip his little finger into it. It's just impossible, they all said and then gave up.

But in the village of N'Diour, about a day's walk from M'Badane, a young man called Birane did not give up.

"I'll win Penda," he told his friends. "Just you wait and see."

Now the N'Diour villagers were the only people in Kenya who were on good

terms with hyenas. Every Friday, they killed a bull and gave it to the hyenas as a peace offering. Because of this, the hyenas never bothered the villagers or attacked their animals or stole their food.

Birane killed an ox, dried the meat, and stuffed it into a goatskin. He wrapped a thick cotton bag around the skin, then hid the whole thing inside a bundle of straw, which he tied up securely with lianas. The very next day was Friday, and when Bouki the Hyena came to get his share of the bull meat, Birane approached him with the bundle.

"Wise Bouki, I have a problem. My messenger—who has no more brains than a flea—has brought back the splendid gifts I sent to Penda's father, Mor of M'Badane, for her dowry. I am sure that if you were to take him this bundle of straw and say, in your charmingly husky voice, 'Birane asks for your daughter's hand in marriage,' he'll say yes straightaway. Would you do me this favor?"

Bouki growled several times until his voice was good and husky.

"I'd be delighted," he answered, "but I'm having a little trouble with my back

and I don't think I could manage that bundle, even though I'm sure it's light as a feather. However, my eldest, M'Bar, is fit and strong. His voice is nearly as husky as mine, and though I say it myself, he is nearly as wise too. He'll do it, and I'm sure he can win Penda for you."

So early next morning, before the sun had risen, Birane tied the bundle onto M'Bar's back, and the hyena trotted off toward M'Badane. After a while, the dew had soaked through the straw, the cotton bag, and the goatskin to the dried meat inside, and the smell of raw meat began to waft into the air. M'Bar stopped, raised his snout, and sniffed, first to the left and then to the right. He was sure he had caught a whiff of meat, but where was it? He walked on, but it wasn't long before he had to stop again. This time he had definitely smelled meat, and it was coming from somewhere nearby. He left the path and sniffed behind bushes, in tussocks of grass, and along cattle tracks, but he couldn't find it. Sometimes he thought the smell was coming from behind him, sometimes in front. But no matter how hard he sniffed and searched, he could not find the meat.

Three days later, M'Bar slunk into the village of M'Badane in a bad temper. He had forgotten all about delivering the message in his best husky voice. Now all he could think of was the tantalizing smell that at the present seemed to be coming from the huts on either side of him. When he reached Mor's home, he didn't bother with the usual greeting. He simply hung his head and mumbled, "Birane of N'Diour said to give you this bundle. He wants to marry your daughter."

Mor took a knife and cut the liana ropes so that the bundle slid off M'Bar's back. He sliced into the straw, pulled out the cotton bag, and unwrapped it. Then he opened up the goatskin and took out the dried meat.

M'Bar's tail started to twitch with rage as he realized what he had been smelling the whole time. He was tempted to snatch a large chunk of the meat and run, but too many of the villagers gathered around had hunting spears.

M'Bar turned away in disgust, and as he walked out of the village he could hear Mor shouting, "Tell your master, Birane, who is clever enough to outwit a hyena, that he can have my daughter."

It took M'Bar three more days to get back to N'Diour, since he stopped at every bundle of straw he encountered along the way back and tore it apart. There were many bundles, because farmers had a habit of tying up straw and leaving it in the fields to collect later. M'Bar scattered straw all over the ground, but he never found a shred of meat or even a sliver of bone.

When the hyena finally dragged himself into N'Diour, Birane came running out of his hut.

"What in heaven's name happened, M'Bar? Why has it taken you six days to deliver my message?"

"None of your business," snapped M'Bar.

"All you need to know is that you can have Mor's daughter."

And before Birane even had time to thank him, M'Bar walked out of the village. Birane could see him heading toward some bundles of straw that had been stacked up in the corner of a field.

Birane never did discover what had taken M'Bar so long, but from that day on, none of the hyenas ever ran errands again for any of the people of N'Diour, or, indeed, for any people anywhere.

# THE WISE MAN'S STORY

◈

A LONG TIME AGO THERE WAS A MAN WHO WAS so wise that whenever there was a serious dispute anywhere in Kenya he was called to act as judge. He became very rich and acquired much land. But even so, he was always kind and fair and never turned away anyone who asked for his help.

When he was old and realized that he did not have long to live, he asked his six sons to his house. They all came, and they sat on the ground around him, waiting to hear his news.

"My sons," he began, "before I die, I want to tell you about three cows that lived in our forests long ago."

"But, Father," interrupted the eldest son, "we thought you wanted to speak to us about something important. Why are you telling us about cows?"

"Patience, dear boy," replied his father. "These cows are very important. You'll see why. Just listen to my story.

"Long ago, cows were wild, meat-eating animals, living and hunting in the forest like all the other beasts. But after many years of being attacked by ferocious lions and leopards, they decided that the forest was not the place for them and that they had better ask humans for protection. The humans agreed to look after them, and so the cows left the forest and became grazing animals.

"But one family of cows decided to stay behind. These three sisters, Ndune, Nyange, and Nguno, stuck together day and night. Ndune had dark red fur and horns that were as sharp as spears. She was fearless and charged at any animal that looked the slightest bit fierce. It was Ndune who would lead the way when the three of them were walking through a part of the forest they did not know. The second sister, Nyange, was pure white, from the tops of her ears to the tip of her swishing tail. She too had strong, pointed horns, but she was careful to use them only when she was attacked. The third sister, Nguno, had no horns. This would have been bad for her, but many of the other animals assumed that because she was hornless, she had magical powers. So they left her alone. Besides, Nguno's sisters were always ready to defend her with their horns.

"The sisters had worked out a very successful hunting technique: Whenever they spotted a possible meal, Ndune would walk ahead and hide behind a bush. Then Nyange and Nguno would charge the creature from behind and chase it toward Ndune, who would leap out just as the fleeing animal reached her hiding place. With a quick thrust of her sharp horns, Ndune would fell and kill the animal in a matter of seconds. Then all three would help themselves to the carcass, eating their fill side by side.

"Now Lion had tried to catch these three sisters many times, to make a meal for himself. He realized that he would only be able to corner one of the cows if he first separated her from her sisters. As long as the three stayed together, he could never overpower any one of them.

"One day, by a stroke of luck, Lion caught sight of Ndune grazing at a short distance from her sisters, so he crept up silently and greeted her.

" 'Sister Ndune,' he growled. 'How beautifully your red coat glows in the sunlight today.'

" 'Oh, Lion,' Ndune replied, 'You startled me. I was just having a peaceful meal here by myself.'

"'Indeed. I can imagine how annoying it must be for you to have to look out for your sisters all the time. With your looks and your magnificent horns, you'd be much better off on your own. I'm sure you even could become queen of the jungle. It's only because of your weakling sisters that you are attacked—no one would dare touch you if you were by yourself.'

"Now Ndune was greatly taken with the idea of all the other animals looking up to her, apart from Lion himself, of course.

"'Do you really think I could become queen?' she asked.

"'No doubt at all,' said Lion. 'Think it over.' And he trotted off, smiling to himself.

"For the next few days, Lion watched the sisters' movements, and at last he spotted Nyange on her own.

"'Sister Nyange,' he said, bowing his head slightly as he approached her. 'Let me congratulate you on your immaculate white coat. I always have admired its brightness, but today it shines as radiantly as the moon itself. I have observed you and your sisters these past few weeks, and it saddens me to see your talents wasted because of them.'

"'What you mean, Lion? I love my sisters very much.'

"'Of course you do, Nyange, and you are always trying to keep the peace

between them. I've seen you try to prevent Ndune from leading you into danger and try to protect Nguno when she wanders too far away. You're a natural peacemaker, you know, and I would very much like you to be chief advisor when animals come to me with their disputes. They would all respect your gleaming white coat, even before you uttered a single word of advice.'

"Now Nyange was very impressed with Lion's proposal and delighted that he considered her suitable for the job.

"'Do you really think I could become chief advisor?' she asked politely.

"'No doubt at all,' replied Lion. 'Think it over.' And he trotted off, grinning to himself.

"The very next day, Lion saw Nguno on her own and called out to her quietly, so as not to frighten her.

"'Sister Nguno,' he said. 'You look so elegant without the clumsy horns that both your sisters wear. But I do so worry about you. I know that other animals often try to attack you. Do you realize that you would have a much more peaceful life without your sisters? They taunt tigers and leopards with their gaudy coats and show-off horns. You could come and live under my protection, and you could be my queen's lady-in-waiting.'

"Nguno, who had been called ugly so often, was flattered to be considered elegant. She also liked the idea of a quiet life under Lion's protection.

"'Do you really think I could become your queen's lady-in-waiting?' she asked.

"'No doubt at all,' replied Lion, and seeing that Nguno had believed every word he had said, he beamed.

"Come, Sister Nguno, come and meet my queen and we can make the arrangements."

"Nguno followed him through the trees. But when they were just out of earshot of her sisters, Lion turned on her and killed her instantly.

"Meanwhile, Nyange had sneaked away from Ndune to look for Lion. She had decided that she wanted to be chief advisor. Lion, who was gnawing on a bone, leapt up as though to greet her—but jumped at her throat instead, and in a minute she, too, was dead.

"Now that Ndune was on her own, it was easy for Lion to surprise her. The

very next day he found her resting by the riverbank. She was very tired because she had been looking for her sisters all night. But before Ndune had time to get to her feet, Lion sprang out from a bush and sunk his teeth into her neck, killing her instantly."

The wise man paused. He had come to the end of his story. He looked at his sons, and from their expressions he knew they had understood what he was trying to tell them. He smiled contentedly. Then the eldest son got to his feet.

"I see now, Father, why you told us about the cows. If they had stayed together, helping and protecting one another, Lion wouldn't have been able to kill them. As the eldest of your sons, I promise you that we will always try to work together and keep this family strong and happy."

The wise man nodded. It had been a good story.